ISBN: 978-1-68489-949-4

Any references to historical events, real people, or real places are used fictitiously. Names, characters, and faces are products of the author's imagination.

Ivory Leonard IV
Self Published
sankofa1619.production@gmail.com
Website: www.sankofa1619.com

Printed by Amazon, in the United States of America.
First printing Edition 2021.

Illustrations by Saeed Briscoe.
Saeedsvpllc@gmail.com
SaeedsVP.net

3

About the Author

Ivory Leonard IV

CEO | Founder of Sankofa1619, LLC
Website: www.sankofa1619.com

In Reconnecting to our Truth, with Book I of the Sankofa1619 Series: "Who Can I Be?", we began this Journey in exploring A New World, career paths, and being reminded that, "These are only jobs, just jobs, not me". Book I deflated the ideas that subjugates us to roles that solely confine us to the working class, while reinstating that we are far much more than an occupation.

To Redefine that which has conditioned us, Book II of the Sankofa1619 Book Series, has a strong emphasis on: Expansion of the Mind.

After the Emancipation Proclamation, the laws replaced the slave master, which limited us to ideas that don't belong to us, while the system continues to flourish from our labor. In discovering these new realms, we continue to shed light on exploration, which defies the restrictions that have confined us. These ideas are still prevalent. Like the slave master, the plantation evolved.

As the Cradle of Civilization, and explorers by Nature, "Where Can I Go?" reminds us that we can go beyond any idea that limits us. In Reclaiming our past, as Originators of human conditioning, this isn't new- this is who we are.

As a messenger of Hope and Love, when we Reclaim, Redefine, and Reconnect to our True Self, we defy that which has kept us bound. Once we free our mind, we free that which is confined. Nonetheless, impacting more than just the present, but our future.

In an effort to shift the Paradigm!

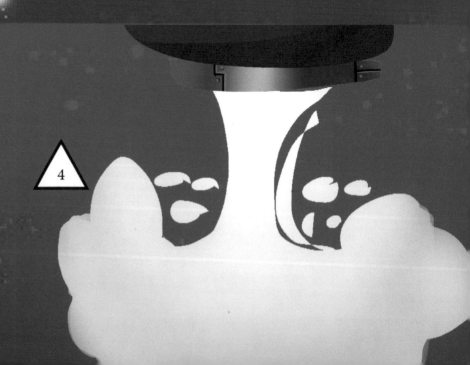

4

Dedicated to the Ancestors
Your Brilliance Lives On...

Where Can I Go?

△ 6

We invite you to explore this world with a concluding activity on page: # 37

7

I want to explore my yard and jump on the grass.
Race a butterfly to see which of us is fast.

Or maybe say, "Hi!," to the Sun at the beach.

As I hear the dolphins talk in their
own speech.

Oh, the places I will go.

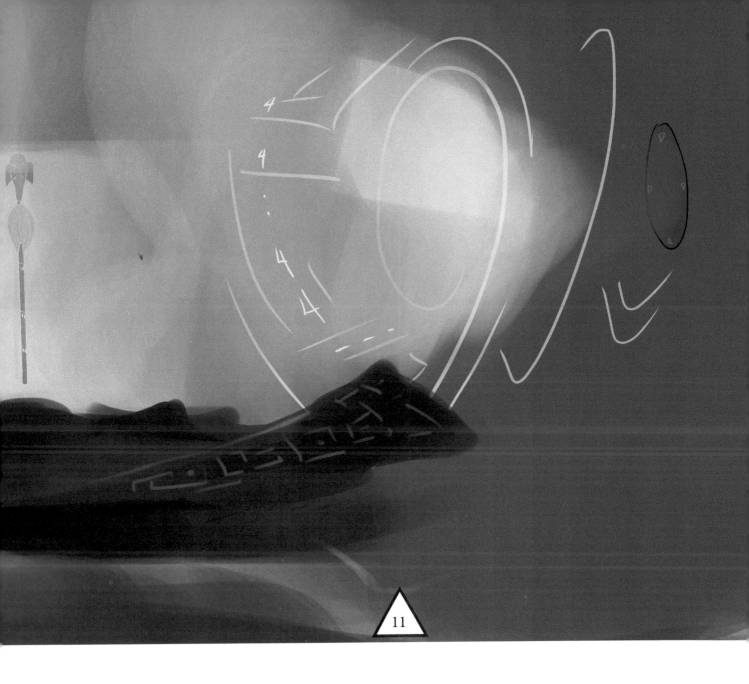

Stand next to the Original People on Mt. Rushmore.

13

14

Or yell in the Canyon to hear my voice roar!!!

Maybe, go to Egypt to see the Pyramids of Giza.

16

Run freely around the tower in France.

On the Great Wall of China, I may do a dance.

Or visit Timbuktu- one of Africa's oldest schools.

Dad said, "this is where most learned," so it must be cool.

I can even time travel to see Ancient Ghana.

Oh, the places I will go? I do wonder.

Let's go to Mars and sing with the stars.

Visit the rings of Saturn- somewhere afar.

Shoot past the moons of Jupiter like a laser beam.

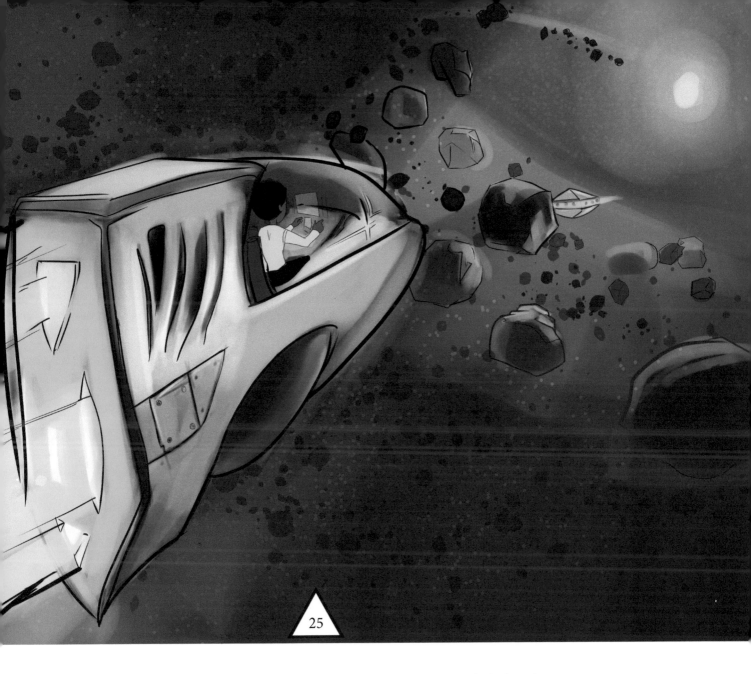

And travel beyond our asteroid belt to
see things no one has seen.

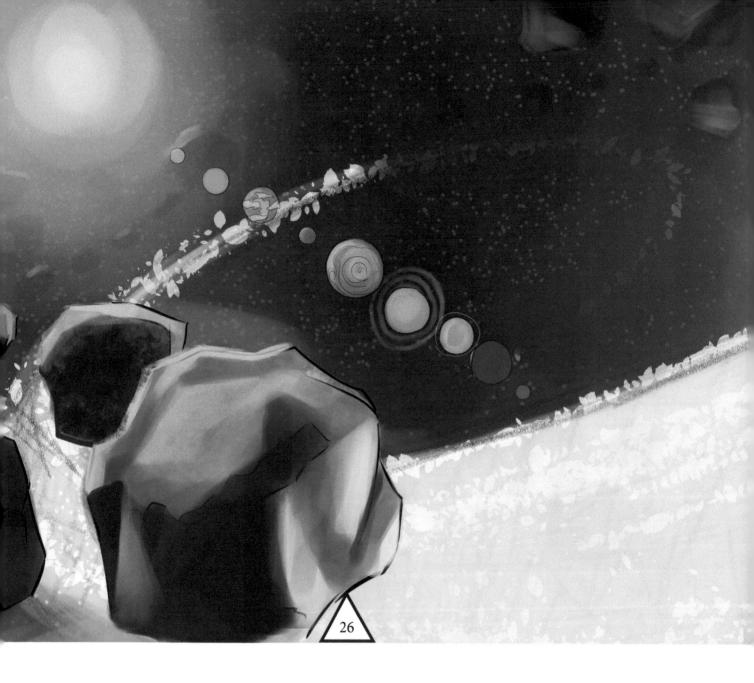

Oh, I wonder, I wonder, where can I go?

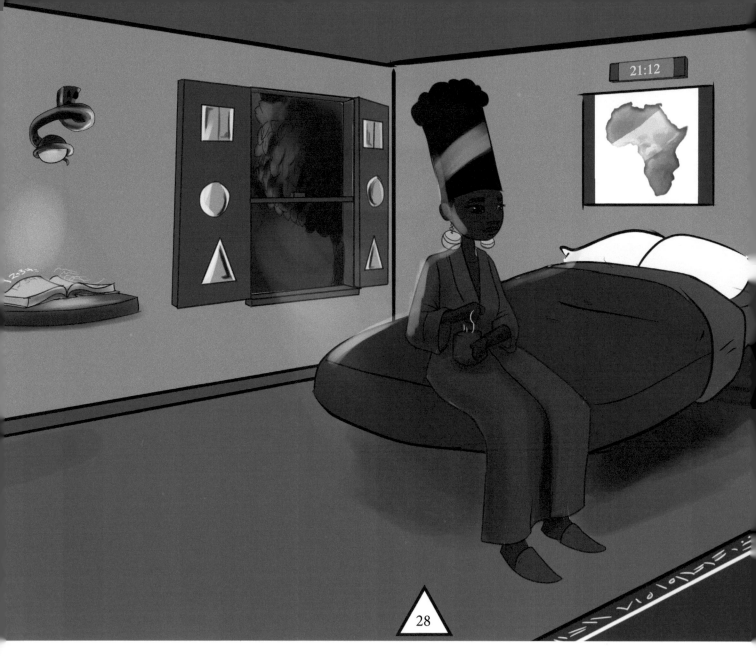

Suddenly, my Mom quietly said,
"Son, you can go anywhere- even to this bed.

Trust, you can, and will, explore the unbound.
Even that which is lost, can always be found.

So, believe in your path and what you create it to be.
And allow no one - even me- deny what you dream.

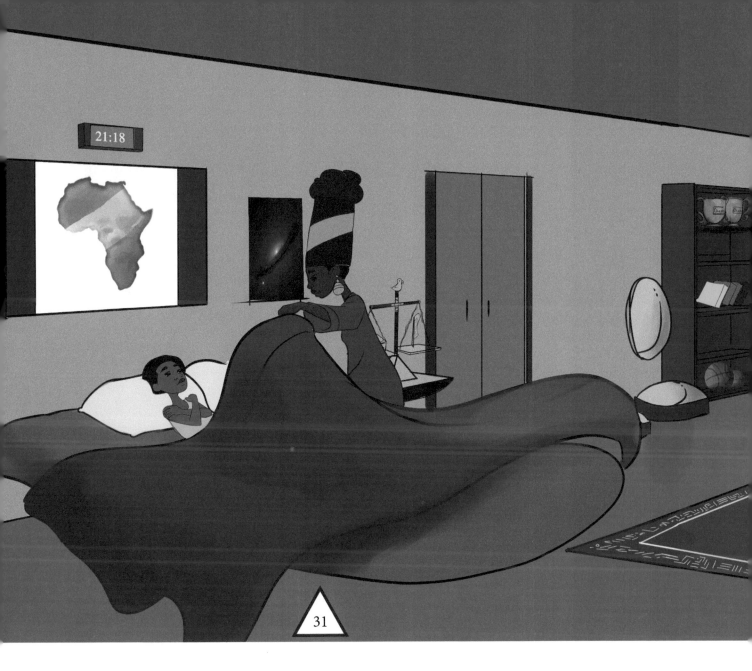

Now, quiet your mind and let your eyes rest.
On tomorrow, you have your addition test."

I closed them slowly without a word to spare.
And dreamt of the places I'll go and the things I'll share.

On tonight, I'll save in my little bank.

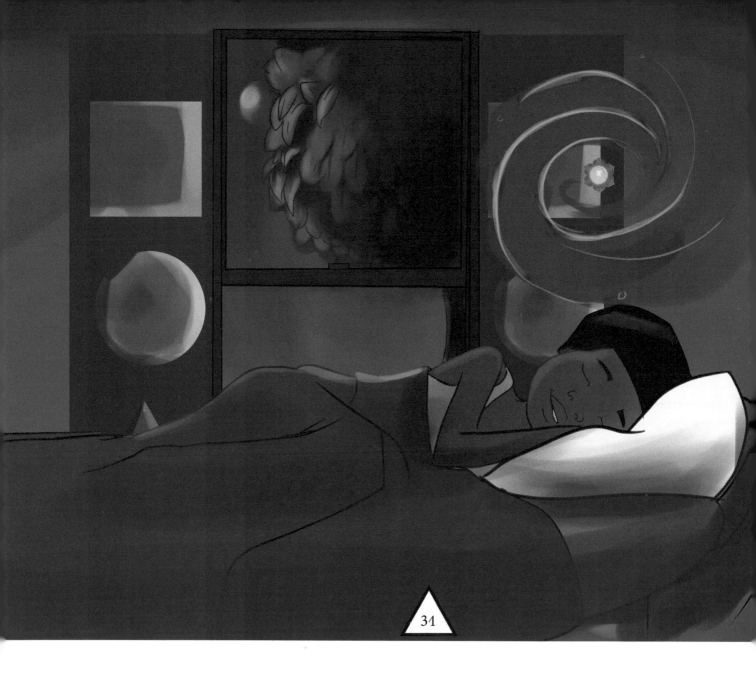

World, here I come! To my vision I thank!

The Journey Continues...

Well Done!

36

(Go to next page for mantras.)

Sacral Mantras

I Am creative.
I Am imaginative.
I Am limitless.

37

Addition Test

1.　3
　　+4

2.　2
　　+6

3.　5
　　+1

4.　4
　　+7

5.　10
　　+3

*Bonus: 3+3+3= _____

38

Treasure Hunt

Questions

1. Locate the page where you can see the Sacral Chakra, which is orange, , and add the page number. _____

2. On page 10, what color is Ahkleem's aura? _____

3. Name the yoga pose Ahkleem is doing on page 8. _____

4. Where are the Pyramids of Giza located? _____

5. Where did Ahkleem time travel to? _____

6. What school does Ahkleem mention on page 18? _____

7. How many moons can you see near Jupiter on page 23? _____

8. On what page can you find the solar panel? _____

9. What is the name of the canyon where you can find graffiti? _____ (hint: "Roar!!!")

10. How many planets are in view on page 26? _____

BONUS: Locate the hidden spacecraft and add the page number. _____

Sacral Chakra- located at the base of the lumbar vertebrae and is connected to the pelvis. Associated with orange. Includes your emotional body and creativity.

Expansion- the action of becoming larger or more extensive.

Upon completion, follow, tag, and repost @sankofa1619 on Instagram with your answers. First 50 with the correct answers will be shared.

△ 39

Sankofa - to go back and get what is lost.

Root Chakra - located at the base of the spine. Associated with the color red. Includes basic needs; such as: food, water, shelter, safety, as well as connection, strength, and fearlessness.

CPSIA information can be obtained
at www.ICGtesting.com
Printed in the USA
BVHW020804200422
634698BV00009BA/757